For Joseph

Willy wouldn’t hurt a fly.

Willy worried about stepping on
tiny insects every time he went
for a walk. When someone knocked
into him, he always said,
"Oh, I'm sorry!"
Even when it wasn't his fault.

Sometimes when he was out walking,
the suburban gorilla gang bullied him.
"Oh, I'm sorry!" said Willy
when they hit him.

The suburban gorillas called him
Willy the Wimp.

Willy hated that name. Willy the Wimp!

One evening when Willy was reading his comic, he saw . . .

That sounds just the thing for me, thought Willy. So he sent some money to the address in the advertisement.

He rushed to the door every morning to catch the postman. "Oh, I'm sorry!" said Willy when the postman brought nothing for him.

But one day a package arrived . . .

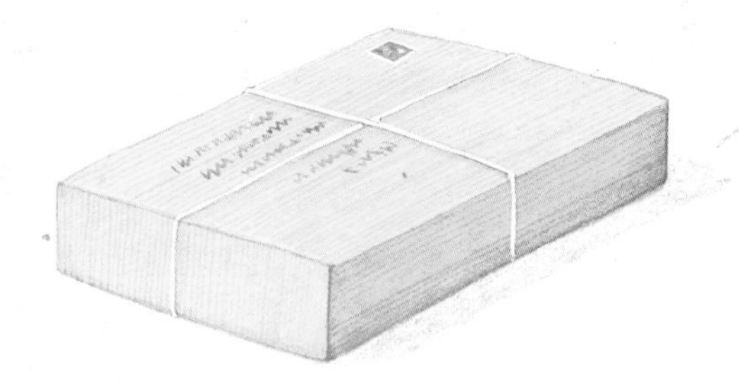

This was it! Willy opened it excitedly. Inside was a book: it told Willy what to do . . .

First some exercises.

Then some jogging.

Willy had to go on a special diet.

He went to aerobics classes
where everybody danced to
disco music. Willy felt a bit silly.

He learned how to box.

And he went to a body-building club.

Willy took up weight lifting, and gradually over weeks and months Willy got bigger . . . and bigger . . .

and bigger . . .

AND BIGGER!

Willy looked in the mirror.
He liked what he saw.

So when Willy walked down the street

and saw the suburban gorillas attacking Millie . . .

They ran.

"Oh . . . Willy," said Millie.
"What, Millie?" said Willy.
"You're my hero, Willy," said Millie.
"Oh . . . Millie," said Willy.

Willy was proud.

"I'm not a wimp!"

A hero.

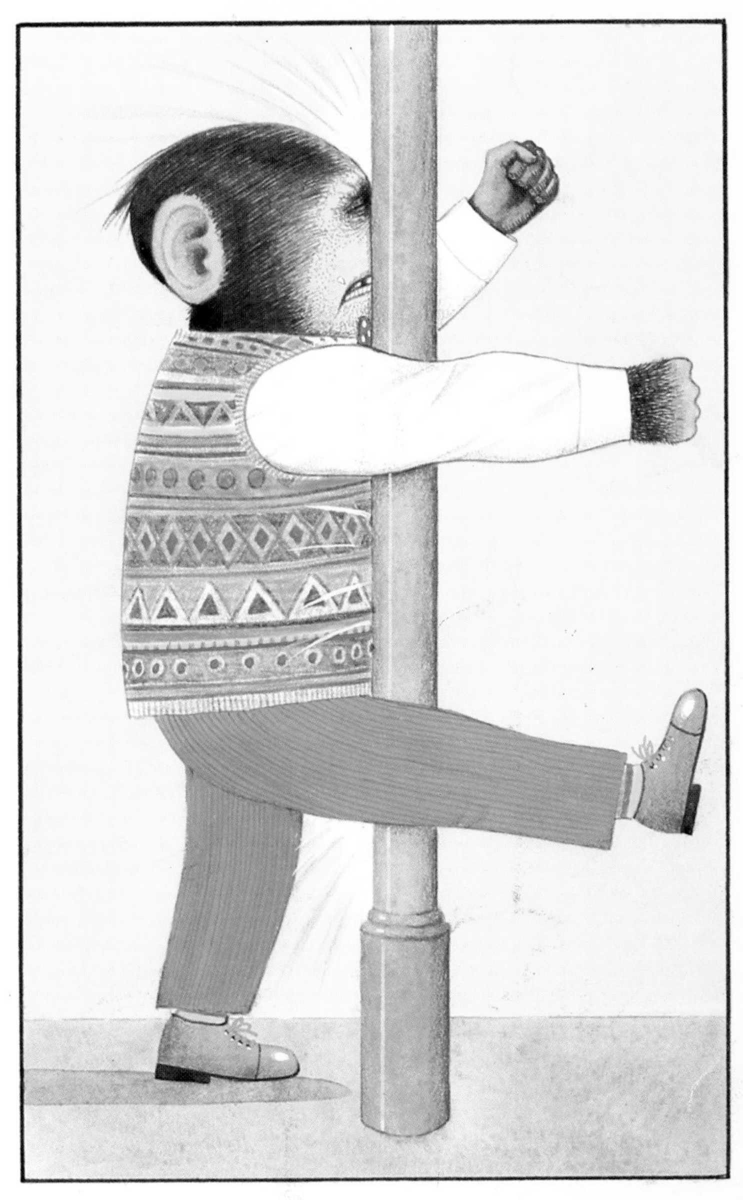

BANG!

"Oh, I'm sorry!" said Willy.